Our Country Is

Dona Herweck Rice

Illustrated by Samya Zitouni

Our country is...

good people of all kinds.

Our country is...

workers and builders.

Our country is...

big cities and small towns.

Our country is...

beaches, mountains, valleys, plains, deserts, and waterways.

Our country is...

towering skyscrapers and buildings low to the ground.

Our country is...
roads and bridges.

Our country is...
well-loved pets and animals in the wild.

Our country is...
historic monuments and museums.

Our country is... national treasures.

Our country is... home sweet home.

Notes for the Grown-ups

This book allows for a rich shared reading experience for children who are early and developing readers. The images help new readers tell the story, either as they read or as they are read to. What a valuable tool for building the confidence new readers need to embark on the adventures that await them while reading!

To extend this reading experience, do one or more of the following:

After reading, come back to the book again and again. Rereading is an excellent tool for building literacy skills.

Learn about the symbols for the United States, such as the flag, a bald eagle, and the White House. Look for the flag in this book.

Ask the child their favorite thing about their country and why.

Talk together about what makes a country. What is important?

How does the child think the author and illustrator of this book feel about the United States? How can they tell?

Consultant
Cynthia Malo, M.A.Ed.

Publishing Credits
Rachelle Cracchiolo, M.S.Ed., *Publisher*
Emily R. Smith, M.A.Ed., *SVP of Content Development*
Véronique Bos, *VP of Creative*
Fabiola Sepulveda, *Art Director*

Library of Congress Cataloging-in-Publication Data
Names: Rice, Dona, author. | Zitouni, Samya, illustrator.
Title: Our country is / Dona Herweck Rice ; illustrated by Samya Zitouni.
Description: Huntington Beach : Teacher Created Materials, Inc., [2025] | Audience: Ages 3-9 | Summary: "Our country is many things. What does it mean to you?"-- Provided by publisher.
Identifiers: LCCN 2024009200 (print) | LCCN 2024009201 (ebook) | ISBN 9798765961384 (paperback) | ISBN 9798765966334 (ebook)
Subjects: LCSH: United States--Juvenile literature. | United States--Pictorial works--Juvenile literature. | LCGFT: Picture books.
Classification: LCC E156 .R524 2025 (print) | LCC E156 (ebook) | DDC 973 [E]--dc23/eng/20240318
LC record available at https://lccn.loc.gov/2024009200
LC ebook record available at https://lccn.loc.gov/2024009201

This book may not be reproduced or distributed in any way without prior written consent from the publisher.

5482 Argosy Avenue
Huntington Beach, CA 92649
www.tcmpub.com
ISBN 979-8-7659-6138-4
© 2025 Teacher Created Materials, Inc.
Printed by: 926
Printed in: Malaysia
PO#: PO11723